Diego Saves a Butterfly

adapted by Lara Bergen
based on the original teleplay by Madellaine Paxson
illustrated by Warner McGee

Ready-to-Read

SIMON SPOTLIGHT/NICK JR.
New York   London   Toronto   Sydney

Based on the TV series *Go, Diego, Go!*™ as seen on Nick Jr.®

SIMON SPOTLIGHT
An imprint of Simon & Schuster Children's Publishing Division
1230 Avenue of the Americas, New York, New York 10020
© 2007 Viacom International Inc. All rights reserved. NICK JR., *Go, Diego, Go!*, and all related
titles, logos, and characters are trademarks of Viacom International Inc.
All rights reserved, including the right of reproduction in whole or in part in any form.
SIMON SPOTLIGHT, READY-TO-READ, and colophon are registered trademarks of
Simon & Schuster, Inc.
Manufactured in the United States of America
First Edition
2 4 6 8 10 9 7 5 3 1
Cataloging-in-Publication Data for this book is available from the Library of Congress.
ISBN-13: 978-1-4169-3364-9
ISBN-10: 1-4169-3364-6

Hi! I am .

DIEGO

Look at this !

COCOON

Do you know what is inside?

It is a  !
BUTTERFLY

It is a Blue Morpho ! BUTTERFLY

"Let me see!" says .

BABY JAGUAR

Oh, no!

The  flew away.

BUTTERFLY

I think

BABY JAGUAR

scared the .

BUTTERFLY

Do not worry, .
BABY JAGUAR

CLICK can help us

find the BUTTERFLY.

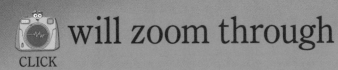  will zoom through

the rainforest to look for

the  .

BUTTERFLY

Is this the ?
BUTTERFLY

No, this is a .
LADYBUG

Is this the ?
BUTTERFLY

Yes!

BUTTERFLIES live
in the rainforest.
But this **BUTTERFLY**
is in a **CAVE**.
The **CAVE** is cold!

We have to bring the  BUTTERFLY

back to the warm rainforest.

Come on!

Now we are in the  CAVE .
But the  CAVE is so dark!
 RESCUE PACK can help us see.

Here is !

RESCUE PACK

Can help us see?

FLIPPERS

No.

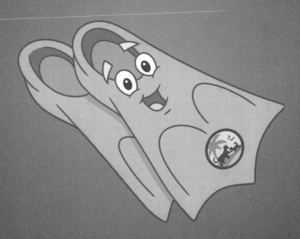

Can a help us see?

FLASHLIGHT

Yes!

There is the  !
BUTTERFLY

"I am too cold to fly," says the  BUTTERFLY.

That is okay, BUTTERFLY.

You can ride with me.

BUTTERFLIES like to sip juice
from **FRUIT** .

Do you see any  ?

FRUIT

"Yum!" says the .
BUTTERFLY

The  was good.
FRUIT

The  is warm
BUTTERFLY

again.

Now she can fly!

To the rainforest!

Come on!

Oh, no!

There is a big  !
BIRD

The  is afraid of  .
BUTTERFLY   BIRDS

When the  BUTTERFLY opens its wings, the BIRD flies away. The BUTTERFLY is brave!

We made it back
to the rainforest.
But where is  ?

BABY JAGUAR

"Here I am," says  .

BABY JAGUAR

"I do not want to scale the .

BUTTERFLY

I want to be friends."

"Me too!" says the .

BUTTERFLY

Thanks for helping us save the ! BUTTERFLY

And thanks for helping make a new friend too!

BABY JAGUAR